Romani and Traveling people throughout the world have a long history. Their culture is based around their language, and their love of story, music and animals. Their tales are passed on from generation to generation, often by word of mouth alone. Despite many challenging times, Travelers have survived and thrived, ready to share their stories with everyone.

Many Travelers do not live in a house on a street, but in homes on wheels instead. They do not go to work in the same building day after day. The woods and fields are their workshops. They make beautiful things, often from recycled objects that others have thrown away, and they trade goods wherever they stop their caravans.

Travelers are hard-working. Wherever they may be, they find a way to turn their talents and efforts into food, clothing and whatever else they need to keep them rolling from place to place.

Ossiri and the Bala Mengro is a tale that celebrates the power and importance of recycling and music within the Traveler community.

To my family

and all the traditional Traveler storytellers – past, present and future

Richard

To my family

Katharine

First published in 2016 by Child's Play (International) Ltd
Ashworth Road, Bridgemead, Swindon SN5 7YD, UK

Published in USA by Child's Play Inc
250 Minot Avenue, Auburn, Maine 04210

Distributed in Australia by Child's Play Australia Pty Ltd
Unit 10/20 Narabang Way, Belrose, Sydney, NSW 2085

ISBN 978-1-84643-925-4
CLP020316CPL04169254

Printed and bound in Shenzhen, China

1 3 5 7 9 10 8 6 4 2

A catalogue record of this book
is available from the British Library

www.childs-play.com

Glossary:

Bala Mengro: *Hairy person* - **Tattin Django**: *Recycling music* - **Daddo**: *Daddy* - **Dordi**: *Oh dear*
Rag-and-bone: *Material for recycling such as cloth, bones, and metals* - **Tattin Folki**: *Rag-and-bone people*

OSSIRI
and the
BALA MENGRO

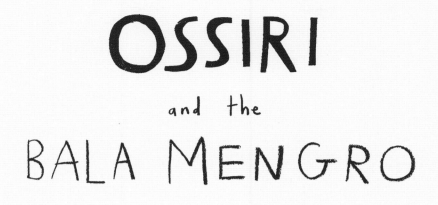

RICHARD O'NEILL • KATHARINE QUARMBY

illustrated by HANNAH TOLSON

Ossiri was a Traveler girl. She and her family worked hard as 'Tattin Folki', or rag-and-bone people, as the settled people called them.

Ossiri's family recycled everything. They sold old clothes that they'd mended and altered, and they turned rags into paper. Old scrap iron was weighed and sold.

Ossiri helped her father and grandfather to load their cart with goods other people had thrown out. Then she led the horse back to the camp so the family could sort through what they had collected.

"I've carved a new leg for that chair, Daddo," she said proudly.
"As good as new, Ossiri!" he replied.
"Better," smiled Mother, as she wove a new seat for the chair.

The whole family loved music, Ossiri especially, who had heard her family singing since she was a babe in arms. When the best Traveler musicians performed at family celebrations, Ossiri couldn't sit still. She would clap her hands, and dance more enthusiastically than anyone else.

"Can I learn to play an instrument?" Ossiri asked
her father one day.

Father shook his head. "We're Tattin Folki, Ossiri,
not musicians. We can't afford to buy you an instrument.
If you were a musician you'd have to travel all over
the country to play, and I need you here with me."

Ossiri couldn't let go of her dream. She yearned to play music.
One afternoon as she sorted through that day's pickings,
listening to the metal clunk and clink, an idea came to her.

"I know! I'll make my own instrument."

She rushed to the woods and cut a long, wide piece of willow.

She shaped it and smoothed it, drilled holes into it and fixed things to it. She stuck on anything that made a good noise – an old piece of scrap from a broken machine, some metal bottle tops and bells. Ossiri called her instrument the Tattin Django.

She struck the Tattin Django hard a few times with a piece of wood and rang the bells. The family ran out of their tents and caravans. Ossiri was delighted to see her audience gather and she took a bow.

But as she straightened up she noticed that the cows in the field nearby were mooing fit to burst, and all the birds had taken flight.

"Ossiri, please stop!" begged her brother. "My ears are hurting."

Ossiri was bitterly disappointed. Her dream of becoming
a famous musician faded as she stowed the Tattin Django
underneath her grandparents' caravan.

"It looks wonderful, Ossiri," said Grandmother, "but it hurt
my old ears. You'll have to get better, my dear, before your
next performance." She patted her gently on the shoulder.

Ossiri squared her shoulders. "I will practice as hard as I can,
Grandmother. I promise."

It was late spring. It was time for them to travel.

"Where are we going this year?" Ossiri asked.

"To Lancashire," said Father. "Lovely country air, plenty of good trade and kind people. But we think you should leave your Tattin Django here."

Ossiri was close to tears.

Grandfather spoke up. "Lancashire is hilly. Ossiri can climb up high and play without disturbing anyone."

After a long journey the family arrived at their new camping ground. They built a fire and cooked an evening meal. Ossiri moved away from the fireside and started to play quietly.

One of the farmer's daughters heard her and put her hands over her ears.

"You don't want to play that around here. If you wake the great ogre you'll be in terrible trouble."

"What's that?" asked Ossiri.

"A huge hairy monster, as tall as a barn. It lives in the cave up there." The girl pointed up the steep hillside. "It loves its sleep and woe betide anyone who wakes it."

She shivered. "Last week my father was plowing the field next to the ogre's cave and the jangling of the harness and the plow blades cutting through the stony soil woke the ogre up. It chased him for hours across hill and dale. That ogre chases anyone who wakes it."

"What would it have done if it had caught him?" asked Ossiri.

"You don't want to know!" said the girl, and walked away.

Ossiri joined her family at the fireside
and told them about the ogre.

"Oh Dordi," exclaimed her father.
"I didn't know the Bala Mengro was still here.
You must be careful."

Ossiri promised that she would
never go into the hills alone.

But she couldn't resist the chance to practice.
The very next day she took her Tattin Django
into the peaks. The sound echoed off the hillside.

As she paused for breath she heard a gigantic yawn.
Ossiri looked around and saw a dark opening
in the hillside, and at the entrance a huge monster.
It was the Bala Mengro – rubbing its large, red eyes.
Ossiri wanted to run but her legs were frozen to the spot.

"I was asleep till you came along!" the Bala Mengro boomed. It was huge, and as hairy as a Shire horse.

"Sorry," Ossiri trembled, shaking from her head to her toes. "I won't wake you again. Please let me go."

"No," growled the Bala Mengro. "You must play for me again!"

Shocked, Ossiri played as loud as she could. The Bala Mengro rumbled, deep and loud. It was singing! The hills shook as the great ogre started to dance.

Eventually, the Bala Mengro stopped dancing and disappeared inside the cave. Ossiri began to tiptoe away, her face white with fear, but she felt its grip on her shoulder. Ossiri froze, but the Bala Mengro just dropped a heavy chain into her hand and walked away.

When she arrived back at the camp, her father looked at the chain. He whistled. "It's solid silver!"

The next day, after finishing her chores, Ossiri went back up into the hills. Again the Bala Mengro danced and sang until it could move no longer. This time it gave Ossiri a gold coin.

Word spread. Many people came to hear Ossiri play.

"Sure enough, it's a terrible sound," said one.

"If it calms the ogre, Ossiri must be doing something right," added another.

No other musician had become so rich so quickly. Ossiri was overjoyed that she was now famed for her musical talent.

One day a stranger arrived. He said
he was a friend of the family, so they
welcomed him to the fireside. He shared
their food and Ossiri admired his shiny
leather boots.

"Which tunes does the ogre like most?" asked the stranger.
Ossiri, who was so proud of her music, told him.

"I hope you keep your instrument hidden safely away,"
said the stranger, earnestly.

"Of course I do," said Ossiri, pointing to a caravan.
"Underneath the steps where no one would look."

That night as Ossiri drifted off to sleep she heard the dogs bark,
but she thought nothing of it.

The next day, when Ossiri went under the caravan
to get her Tattin Django, the instrument had vanished.

"It's gone!" she cried, and her family came running.

They searched far and wide but it was nowhere to be found.

"Why would someone steal my Tattin Django?" Ossiri cried.

Just then the noise of the instrument echoed down the hillside.

Ossiri and Grandfather ran up the hill as fast as they could.
In the distance they could see the stranger trying to play
Ossiri's Tattin Django, the Bala Mengro towering over him.

But when they finally reached the cave, the music had stopped and nobody was there. The Tattin Django lay on the ground, alongside the stranger's boots.

The stranger had asked Ossiri many questions, but he had forgotten to ask why the Bala Mengro liked her music. Perhaps it was because she played from the heart, not for gain.

And so she does, until this day, in very shiny leather boots!